LUATH
Treasury of Scottish Nursery Rhymes

Introduced and compiled by
ALASDAIR HUTTON

with colour-me-in illustrations by
BOB DEWAR

Luath Press Limited
EDINBURGH
www.luath.co.uk

First published 2016
This edition 2023
Reprinted 2024, 2025

ISBN: 978-1-80425-010-5

The paper used in this book is recyclable. It is made from low chlorine pulps produced in a low energy, low emissions manner from renewable forests.

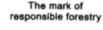

Printed and bound by
Robertson Printers, Forfar

Typeset in 13 point adobe text Pro by 3btype.com

© Luath Press Ltd, 2016

ALASDAIR HUTTON was the writer and narrator of the Royal Edinburgh Military Tattoo from 1992 to 2019 and has written and introduced hundreds of events and concerts in Scotland and around the world. As well as writing the history of the 15th Scottish Volunteer Battalion of the Parachute Regiment, to which he belonged for 22 years, he is the author of two books for children, *The Tattoo Fox* and *The Tattoo Fox Makes New Friends*. He has also published an account of his 25 years writing and narrating The Royal Edinburgh Tattoo – *The Greatest Show on Earth: Behind the Microphone at The Royal Edinburgh Military Tattoo*. He has worked for the BBC in Scotland and Northern Ireland and was Member of the European Parliament for the South of Scotland and Convener of Scottish Borders Council. He lives in the Scottish Borders town of Kelso.

BOB DEWAR was born in Edinburgh at an early age. Sixteen years later he was published nationally. He worked in DC Thomson's studio where, among other things, he ghosted Dennis the Menace. After going freelance, he did political and social commentary for *The Scotsman* newspaper. He has illustrated books for many publishers including the Children's and English Speaking Departments of Oxford University Press, and for Fife Educational Social Development. His work has also appeared in *The Times*, *The Herald*, *Scottish Field* and The Scotch Malt Whisky Society newsletter and on its Members Room ceiling. He has had exhibitions in Lucca, Italy, in Glasgow and in Edinburgh and had caricatures hanging in the House of Commons. He is now a lot older than 16 and is married to the novelist Isla Dewar, with two sons and an absurdly friendly big golden retriever. Bob has no idea how this friendliness happened, since he tends toward grumpiness.

To Fergus Alexander Hutton

Contents

Introduction	13

Lullabies

And hee and ba, birdie	16
Ba, wee birdie, birdie	18
Bye, babie buntin'	20
Dance to your daddie	22
Dingle, dingle dousy	24
Roun', roun' rosie, cuppie, cuppie shell	26
Feetikin, feetikin	27
Here we go up, up, up	28
Hey, my kitten, my kitten	30
Hush-a-ba, babie, lie still, lie still	32
Hush-a-ba birdie, croon, croon	34
Hush-a-bye baby	36
Hush and baloo, babie	38
Hushie-ba, burdie beeton!	39
O can ye sew cushions	39
Rock-a-bye, baby	40
This is the way the ladies ride	42
Wee Davie Daylicht	44

One to Two

Bounce buckram, velvet's dear	49
Ca' Hawkie, drive Hawkie	50
Cam ye by the kirk	52

Deedle, deedle, dumpling	53
Goosey, goosey, gander	54
Haily Paily	56
I had a little pony	57
I've a kisty	58
If all the seas were one sea	60
Ladybird	62
Little Miss Muffet	64
Poussie, poussie, baudrons	66
Sing a sang o' saxpence	68
The cattie rade to Passelet	70
To market, to market, to buy a plum-cake	71
Wee Willie Winkie	72
Young lambs to sell!	76

Two to Three

Babbity-Bowster	80
Cock and Hen	82
Earwig	84
Hannah Bantry in the pantry	86
I Wullie Wastle	88
Jean, Jean, Jean	90
Little Jack Horner	92
Little Tommy Tucker	94
Madam Pussie's coming hame	96
Nieve-Nievie, Nick-Nack	98
Rain, rain, go away	100
Rain, rain rattle stanes	102

Robin, Robin Redbreast	104
See, saw, Margery Daw	106
The bonnie moor-hen	108
The Hunting of the Wren	110
The silly bit chicken!	114
There were two crows sat on a stone	116
Struthill Well	118

Three to Four

Come, let's to bed	122
Four-and-twenty mermaids	124
Four corners to my bed	126
Hey-how for Hallowe'en	126
I saw a ship a-sailing	128
If you sneeze on Monday	130
Jing-a-Ring	132
Katie Beardie	134
Liar, liar, lick-spit	136
Matthew, Mark, Luke and John	138
Och, here's a puir widow frae Babylon	139
Polly put the kettle on	140
The cuckoo is a bonnie bird	142
The Lion and the Unicorn	144
There was a wee wifie rowed up in a blanket	146
What are little boys made of?	148
Your plack and my plack	150

Four to Five

Aiken Drum	154
As I went o'er the Hill o' Hoos	158
Blaw, blaw!	160
He that would thrive	162
How many miles to Glasgow Lea?	164
I had three little sisters across the sea	165
If the evening's red, and the morning gray	167
Mary had a little lamb	168
The moon shines bright (and girls and boys, come out to play)	170
My wheelie goes round	171
Old Mother Hubbard	172
Paddy on the Railway	176
Sticks and Stones	177
Simple Simon met a Pieman	178
The Frog and Mouse	182
The Raven and the Crow	186
Tom, Tom, the Piper's Son	188
Rhymes about the weather	
When cocks gang crawin' to their beds	192
When the wind is in the east	193
When Yule comes, dule comes	194

Five to Six

A man of words and not of deeds	196
Bless the sheep for Dauvid's sake	197
If wishes were horses	198
March said to Averil	200
St Swithin's day, if thou dost rain	202
See a pin and pick it up	204
Tam o' the Linn	206
The Fause Knicht	208
The Fishermen's Song	210
The gunpowder plot	211
The Wee, Wee Man	212
They that wash on Monanday	214
This is the way we go to school	215
When good King David ruled this land	216
When I was a wee thing	217
Wild geese, wild geese	222

Introduction

Every child loves rhythm and the music of words. In every country on earth, children learn these from the moment they are born and most of what they learn comes from the nursery rhymes they hear as they are growing.

From the crooning lullabies and little bouncing rhymes they hear as babies to the happy, repetitive verses they learn as they begin to understand words and to talk themselves, these nursery rhymes are where every child starts.

Because these rhymes were simple, they travelled well and some started life in other places but found their way to Scotland over the years and into the hearts of Scottish children.

The best way for children to learn the sound of the words and the rhythm of the verses is to hear you reading them aloud. If you would also like to download readings which I have made of some of these verses, you can find them on www.luath.co.uk.

In this little book we have gathered some of the best loved of the rhymes which Scottish children have heard for centuries. Most of them are old, some of them are very old, but all of them have weathered the years and shown their staying power and each one has helped to imbue every child who has heard them with a love of the rhythm and music of words.

In this book you will find not just the words but Bob Dewar has brought the old verses to life with the vivid imagination of his drawings.

I am most grateful to all at Luath for making the gathering of this Treasury of Scottish Nursery Rhymes as much of a pleasure as these verses were when I heard them first as a child.

Alasdair Hutton
Kelso

Lullabies

And hee and ba, birdie

And hee and ba, birdie,
And hee and ba, lamb;
And hee and ba, birdie,
My bonny wee lamb!

Ba, wee birdie, birdie

Ba, wee birdie, birdie;
Ba, wee birdie, croon;
The ewes are awa to the siller parks,   *sheep, rented fields*
The kye's amang the broom;   *cows*
The wee bits o' yowes to the heathery knowes,
They'll no be back till noon;
If they dinna get something ere they gang out,
Their wee pipes will be toom.   *throats, empty*

Bye, babie buntin'

Bye, babie buntin',
Your daddie's gane a-huntin';
Your mammie's gane to buy a skin
To row the babie buntin' in.   *wrap*

Dance to your daddie

Dance to your daddie,
My bonnie laddie,
Dance to your daddie, my, bonnie lamb!
And ye'll get a fishie
In a little dishie –
Ye'll get a fishie when the boat comes hame!

Dance to your daddie,
My bonnie laddie,
Dance to your daddie, my bonnie lamb!
And ye'll get a coatie,
And a pair o' breekies –   *breeches = trousers*
Ye'll get a whippie and a supple Tam!
          A spinning top with a whip to make it spin

LULLABIE

A rhyme to bring a smile to a wee face filled with tears or to help a young child fall asleep. Switch on a torch and wave it to and fro in order to produce mesmerising loops of light in the darkness. This used to be done with a burning stick and the rhyme for it was called a dingle dousy.

Dingle, dingle dousy

Dingle, dingle dousy,
The cat's at the well;
The dog's awa to Musselburgh
To buy the bairn a bell.

Greet, greet, bairnie,
And ye'll get a bell,
If ye dinna greet faster,
I'll keep it to mysel'!

Roun', roun' rosie, cuppie, cuppie shell

Roun', roun' rosie, cuppie, cuppie shell,
The dog's awa' to Hamilton, to buy a new bell;
If you dinna tak' it, I'll tak' it to mysel',
Roun', roun' rosie, cuppie, cuppie shell.

Feetikin, feetikin

Feetikin, feetikin,
When will ye gang?
When the nights turn short,
And the days turn lang,
I'll toddle and gang, toddle and gang.

Here we go up, up, up

Here we go up, up, up,
And here we go down, down, downy;
And here we go backwards and forwards,
And here we go round, round, roundy.

Hey, my kitten, my kitten

Hey, my kitten, my kitten,
And hey, my kitten, my deary!
Such a sweet pet as this
Was neither far nor neary.

Hush-a-ba, babie, lie still, lie still

Hush-a-ba, babie, lie still, lie still;
Your Mammie's awa' to the mill, the mill;
Babie is greeting for want of good keeping –
Hush-a-ba, babie, lie still, lie still.

Hush-a-ba birdie, croon, croon

Hush-a-ba birdie, croon, croon,
Hush-a-ba birdie, croon,
The sheep are gane to the silver wood,
And the cows are gane to the broom.

And it's braw milking the kye, kye,
It's braw milking the kye,
The birds are singing, the bells are ringing,
The wild deer come galloping by.

And hush-a-ba birdie, croon, croon,
Hush-a-ba birdie, croon,
The gaits are gane to the mountain hie,   *goats*
And they'll no be hame till noon, noon.

Hush-a-bye baby

Hush-a-bye baby on the tree top,
When the wind blows the cradle will rock.
When the bough breaks the cradle will fall,
And down will come cradle and baby and all.

Hush and baloo, babie

Hush and baloo, babie,
Hush and baloo;
A' the lave's in their beds –   *All the rest are in their beds*
I'm hushin' you.

Hushie-ba, burdie beeton!

Hushie-ba, burdie beeton!
Your mammie's gane to Seaton,
For to buy a lammie's skin,
To wrap your bonnie boukie in.   *body*

O can ye sew cushions

O can ye sew cushions,
Can ye sew sheets,
Can ye sing Ba-loo-loo,
When the bairn greets?   *baby cries*

Rock-a-bye, baby

Rock-a-bye, baby, thy cradle is green;
Father's a nobleman, mother's a queen;
And Betty's a lady, and wears a gold ring;
And Johnny's a drummer, and drums for the king.

This is the way the ladies ride

This is the way the ladies ride,
Jimp and sma', jimp and sma'
This is the way the gentlemen ride,
Trotting a', trotting a';
This is the way the cadgers ride,
Creels and a'! Creels and a'!!
Creels and a'!!!

Wee Davie Daylicht
1874, Robert Tennant 1830–1879

Wee Davie Daylicht
Keeks o'er the sea   *peeps*
Early in the morning
Wi' a clear e'e;
Waukens a' the birdies
That were sleepin' soun'
Wee Davie Daylicht
Is nae lazy loon.   *boy*

Wee Davie Daylicht
Glowers o'er the hill   *gazes*
Glints through the greenwood,
Dances on the rill;
Smiles on the wee cot,
Shines on the ha'
Wee Davie Daylicht
Cheers the hearts o' a'.

Come, bonnie bairnie
Come awa to me;
Cuddle in my bosie,   *bosom*
Sleep upon my knee;
Wee Davie Daylicht
Noo has closed his e'e
In among the rosy clouds
Far ayont the sea.   *Beyond*

One to Two

Bounce buckram, velvet's dear

Bounce buckram, velvet's dear;
Christmas comes but once a year.

Ca' Hawkie, drive Hawkie

Ca' Hawkie, drive Hawkie,
Ca' Hawkie through the water,
Hawkie is a sweer beast, *unwilling*
And Hawkie winna wade the water; *will not*
But I'll cast aff my hose and shoon, *socks and shoes*
And I'll drive Hawkie through the water.

Cam ye by the kirk

Cam ye by the kirk,
Cam ye by the steeple?
Saw ye our guidman
Riding on a ladle?
Foul fa' the body,
Winna buy a saddle,
Wearing a' his breeks,
Riding on a ladle!

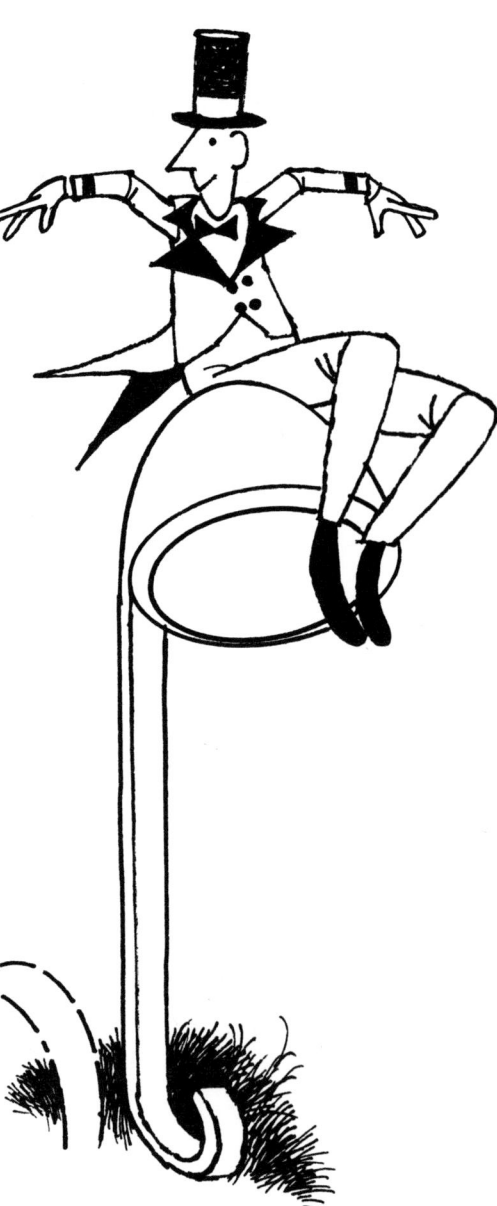

Deedle, deedle, dumpling

Deedle, deedle, dumpling, my son John
Went to bed with his trousers on;
One shoe off, the other shoe on,
Deedle, deedle, dumpling,
 my son John.

Goosey, goosey, gander

Goosey, goosey, gander,
Whither shall I wander?
Upstairs and downstairs,
And in my lady's chamber.
There I meet an old man
Who would not say his prayers;
So I took him by the left leg,
And threw him down the stairs.

Haily Paily

Haily Paily,
Sits on the sands,
Combs her hair
With her lily-white hands.

I had a little pony

I had a little pony,
Its name was Dapple Grey
I lent it to a lady,
To ride a mile away.
She whipped it, she lashed it,
She ca'd it owre the brae
I winna lend my pony mair,
Though a' the ladies pray.

ONE TO TWO

I've a kisty

I've a kisty,
I've a creel,
I've a baggie
Full of meal.

I've a doggie
At the door,
One, two,
Three, four.

If all the seas were one sea

If all the seas were one sea,
What a great sea that would be!
And if all the trees were one tree,
What a great tree that would be!
And if all the axes were one axe,
What a great axe that would be!
And if all the men were one man,
What a great man he would be!
And if the great man took the great axe,
And cut down the great tree,
And let it fall into the great sea,
What a splish splash that would be!

Ladybird

Lady, Lady Landers,
Lady, Lady Landers,
Take up your cloak
About your head,
And fly away
To Flanders.

Fly o'er firth,
And fly o'er fell,
Fly o'er pool,
And running well,
Fly o'er moor,
And fly o'er mead,
Fly o'er living,
Fly o'er dead.

Fly o'er corn,
And fly o'er lea,
Fly o'er river,
Fly o'er sea,
Fly you east,
Or fly you west,
Fly to him
That loves me best.

Little Miss Muffet

Little Miss Muffet
Sat on a tuffet,
Eating her curds and whey;
There came a spider,
And sat down beside her,
And frightened Miss Muffet away.

Poussie, poussie, baudrons

Poussie, poussie, baudrons,   *names for cats*
Where hae ye been?
I've been at London,
Seeing the queen!

Poussie, poussie, baudrons,
What got ye there?
I got a guid fat mousikie,
Rinning up a stair!

Poussie, poussie, baudrons,
What did ye do wi't?
I put it in my meal-poke   *bag for oatmeal*
To eat it to my bread!

Sing a sang o' saxpence

Sing a sang o' saxpence,
A baggie fu' o' rye,
Four-and-twenty blackbirds,
Bakit in a pie.
When the pie was opened
The birds began to sing
And wasna that a dainty dish
To set before the King?

The king was in his counting-house
Counting out his money,
The Queen was in the parlour
Eating bread and honey,
The maid was in the garden
Hanging out the clothes,
When by came a blackbird
And snapped aff her nose.

The cattie rade to Passelet

The cattie rade to Passelet,   *an old name for Paisley*
To Passelet, to Passelet;
The cattie rade to Passelet,
Upon a harrow tine, O.   *one of the prongs of a harrow*

'Twas on a weetie Wednesday,
Wednesday, Wednesday;
'Twas on a weetie Wednesday,
I missed it aye sin-syne, O.

To market, to market, to buy a plum-cake

To market, to market, to buy a plum-cake;
Back again, back again, baby is late;
To market, to market, to buy a plum-bun,
Back again, back again, market is done.

Wee Willie Winkie

1842, William Miller 1810–1872

Wee Willie Winkie rins through the toon,
Upstairs and Doonstairs in his nichtgoon.
Chappin' at the windaes, crying at the lock
'Are all the bairnies in their beds, it's past eight o'clock?'

Hey, Willie Winkie, are you coming ben?
The cat's singing grey thrums to the sleeping hen. *purring*
The dog's speldered on the floor and doesn't give a cheep,
But here's a wakeful laddie that winnna fall asleep.

Onything but sleep, you rogue, glowering like the moon,
Rattling in an iron jug with an iron spoon,
Rumbling, tumbling, round about, crowing like a cock,
Skirling like a kenna-whit, waking sleeping folk.   *Shrill screaming*

Hey, Willie Winkie, the wean's in the creel!   *baby*
Wambling off a body's knee like a very eel,   *wriggling*
Tugging at the cat's ear, raveling all her thrums
Hey Willie Winkie, see, there he comes!

Wearied is the mither that has a storrie wean,
A wee stumpie stoussie, that canna rin his lane, *short, stout, by himself*
That has a battle aye wi' sleep before he'll sloe an e'e *shut an eye*
But a kiss frae aff his rosy lips gi'es strength anew tae me.

Young lambs to sell!

Young lambs to sell!
Young lambs to sell!
If I'd as much money as I can tell,
I never would cry,
Young lambs to sell!

Two to Three

Babbity-Bowster

Wha learned you to dance,
Babbity-Bowster, Babbity-Bowster?
Wha learned you to dance,
Babbity-Bowster, brawly?

My minnie learned me to dance,
Babbity-Bowster, Babbity-Bowster.
My minnie learned me to dance,
Babbity-Bowster, brawly.

Who gave you the keys to keep,
Babbity-Bowster, Babbity-Bowster?
Who gave you the keys to keep,
Babbity-Bowster, brawly?

My minnie gave me the keys to keep,
Babbity-Bowster, Babbity-Bowster.
My minnie gave me the keys to keep,
Babbity-Bowster, brawly.

Cock and Hen

Ilka day,
An egg I lay,
And yet I aye go barefoot,
Barefoot.

I've been through all the toon,
Seeking you a pair of shoon;
Would you have my heart out,
Heart out?

Earwig

The horny goloch is an awesome beast,
Supple and scaly;
It has twa horns, and a hantle of feet,
And a forkie tailie.

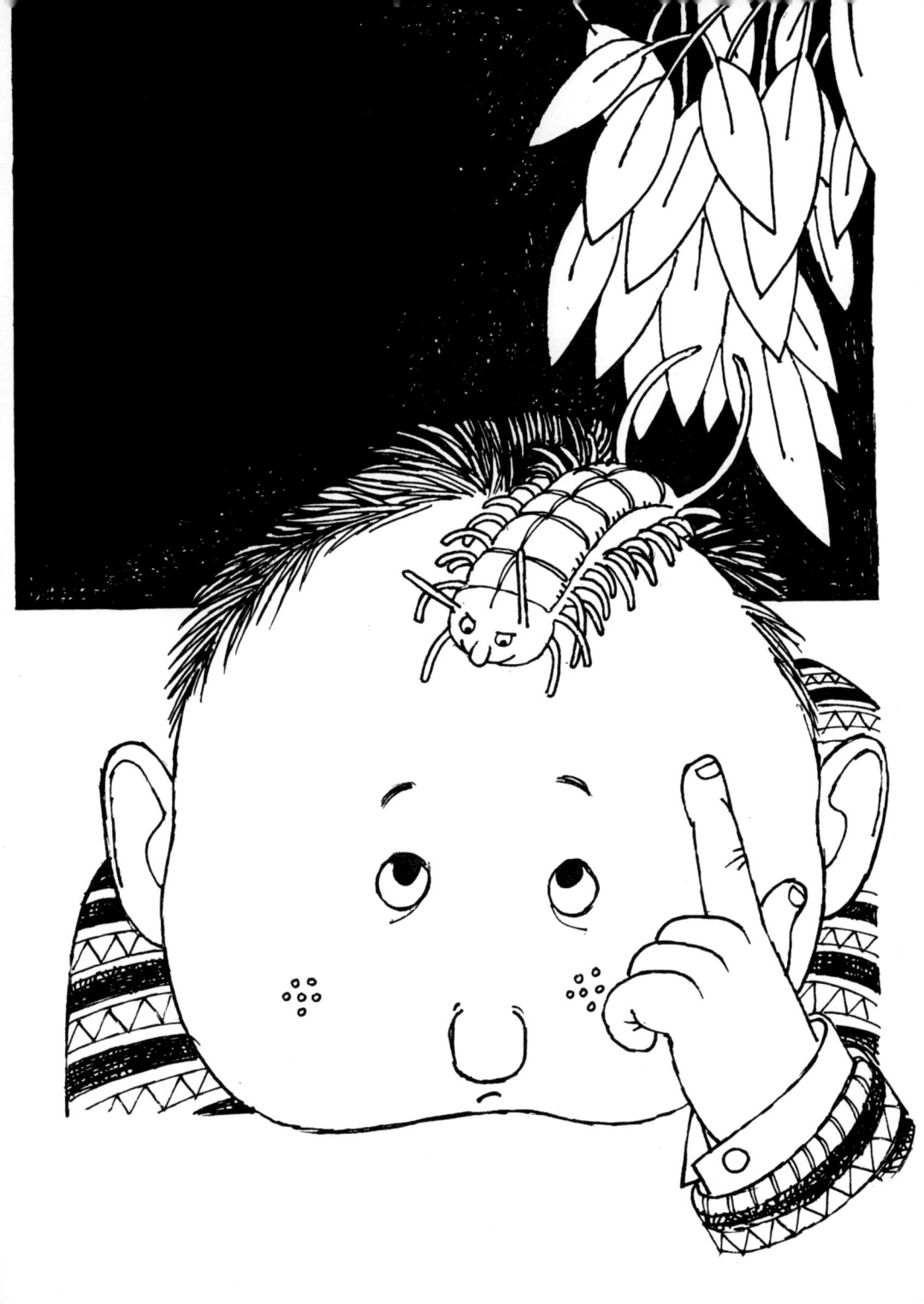

Hannah Bantry in the pantry

Hannah Bantry in the pantry,
Eating a mutton bone;
How she gnawed it, how she clawed it,
When she was alone!

PANTRY

I Wullie Wastle

I Wullie Wastle
Stand here on ma Castle;
An' a' the dogs o' your toon,
Will never drive Wullie Wastle doon!

Jean, Jean, Jean

Jean, Jean, Jean,
The cat's at the cream,
Supping with her forefeet,
And glowering with her een.

Little Jack Horner

A 16th century rhyme

Little Jack Horner
Sat in a corner
Eating his Christmas pie
He put in his thumb
And pulled out a plum,
And said, What a good boy am I.

Little Tommy Tucker

Little Tommy Tucker
Sings for his supper;
What shall he eat?
White bread and butter.

How shall he cut it,
Without e'er a knife?
How will he be married
Without e'er a wife?

Madam Pussie's coming hame

Madam Pussie's coming hame,
Riding on a grey stane.
What's to the supper?
Pease brose and butter.

Who'll say the grace?
I'll say the grace.
Leviticus, Levaticus,
Taste, taste, taste!

Nieve-Nievie, Nick-Nack

Nieve-nievie, nick-nack,
Whit haun will ye tak?
Tak the richt, tak the wrang,
I'll beguile ye gin I can.   *if*

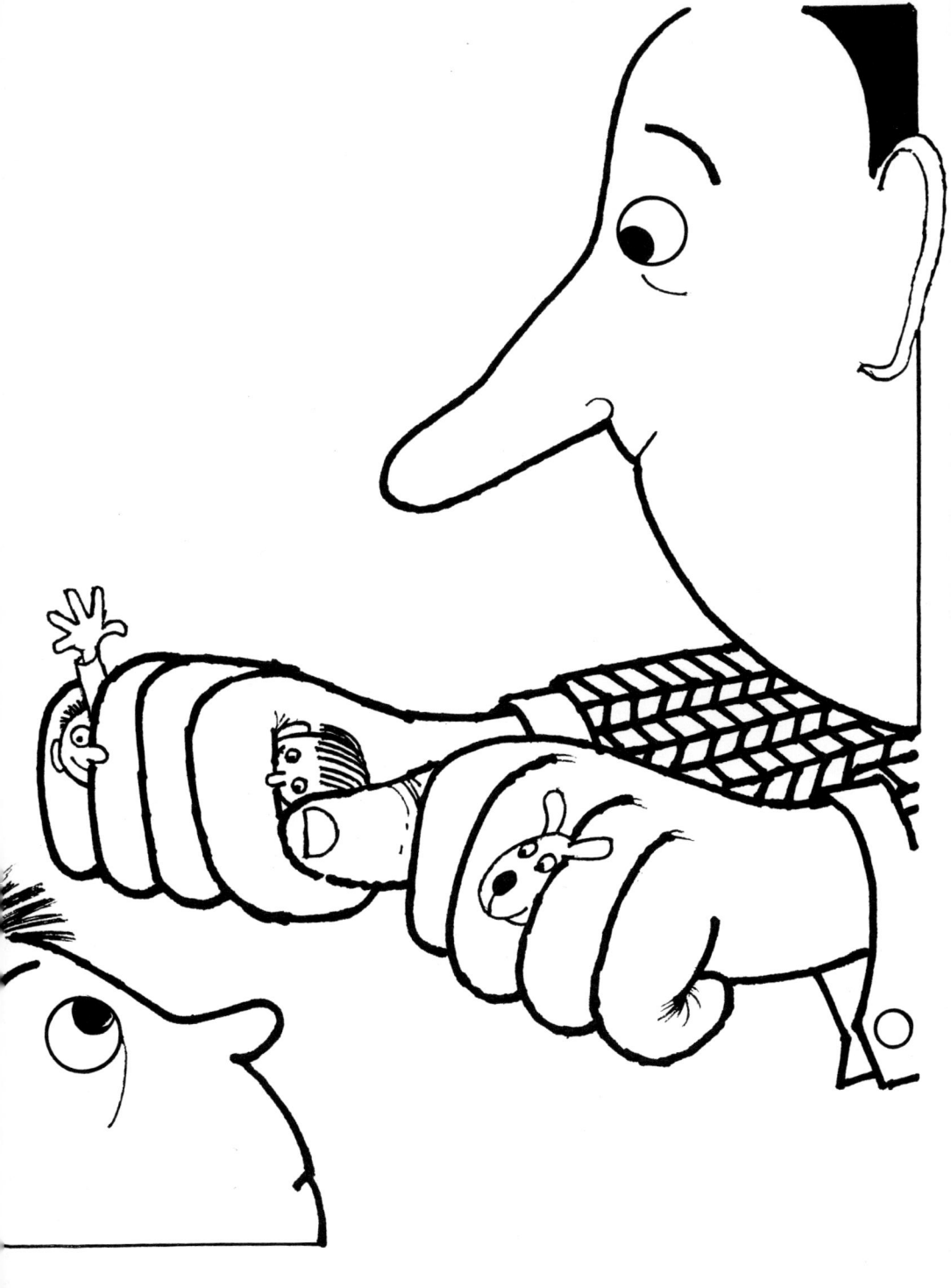

Rain, rain, go away

Rain, rain, go away;
Come again another day;
Little Arthur wants to play.

Rain, rain, rattle stanes

Rain, rain, rattle stanes,
Do not rain on me;
But rain on John o' Groats' house
Far o'er the sea.

Robin, Robin Redbreast

Robin, Robin Redbreast,
Cutty, cutty wran, *short, wren*
Gin you harry my nest,
You'll never be a man.

Robin, Robin Redbreast
Sits upon a rail;
He nods with his head,
And wags with his tail.

See, saw, Margery Daw

See, saw, Margery Daw
Johnny shall have a new master;
He shall have but a penny a day,
Because he can't work any faster.

The bonnie moor-hen

The bonnie moor-hen
Has feathers enou
The bonnie moor-hen
Has feathers enou.

There's some of them black,
And there's some of them blue,
The bonnie moor-hen
Has feathers enou.

The Hunting of the Wren

Will you go to the wood? quo Fozie Mozie;
Will you go to the wood? quo Johnie Rednosie;
Will you go to the wood? quo Fozlin Ene;
Will you go to the wood? quo brother and kin.

What to do there? quo Fozie Mozie;
What to do there? quo Johnie Rednosie;
What to do there? quo Fozlin Ene;
What to do there? quo brother and kin.

To slay the Wren, quo Fozie Mozie;
To slay the Wren, quo Johnie Rednosie;
To slay the Wren, quo Fozlin Ene;
To slay the Wren, quo brother and kin.

What way will you get her hame? quo Fozie Mozie;
What way will you get her hame? quo Johnie Rednosie;
What way will you get her hame? quo Fozlin Ene;
What way will you get her hame? quo brother and kin.

We'll hire cart and horse, quo Fozie Mozie;
We'll hire cart and horse, quo Johnie Rednosie;
We'll hire cart and horse, quo Fozlin Ene;
We'll hire cart and horse, quo brother and kin.

What way will you get her in? quo Fozie Mozie;
What way will you get her in? quo Johnie Rednosie;
What way will you get her in? quo Fozlin Ene;
What way will you get her in? quo brother and kin.

We'll drive down the door-cheeks, quo Fozie Mozie;   *door-posts*
We'll drive down the door-cheeks, quo Johnie Rednosie;
We'll drive down the door-cheeks, quo Fozlin Ene;
We'll drive down the door-cheeks, quo brother and kin.

I'll have a wing, quo Fozie Mozie;
I'll have another, quo Johnie Rednosie;
I'll have a leg, quo Fozlin Ene;
And I'll have another, quo brother and kin.

The hunting of the wren goes on to this day in the Isle of Man.

The silly bit chicken!

The silly bit chicken!
Gar cast her a pickle,
And she'll grow mickle,
And she'll grow mickle.

And she'll grow mickle,
And she'll do good,
And lay an egg
To my little brood.

There were two crows sat on a stone

There were two crows sat on a stone,
Fal de ral,
One flew away and there remained one,
Fal de ral,
The other seeing his neighbour gone,
Fal de ral,
He flew away and there was none,
Fal de ral.

Struthill Well

Three white stones,
And three black pins,
Three yellow gowans   *daisies*
Off the green,
Into the well,
With a one, two, three,
And a fortune, a fortune,
Come to me.

Three to Four

Come, let's to bed

Come, let's to bed,
Says Sleepy-head;
'Tarry a while,' says Slow;
'Put on the pot,'
Says Greedy-gut,
'Let's sup before we go.'

Four-and-twenty mermaids

Four-and-twenty mermaids,
Who left the port of Leith,
To tempt the fine old hermit,
Who dwelt upon Inchkeith.

No boat, no waft, nor crayer,   *wind, wheelhouse*
Nor craft had they, nor oars nor sails;
Their lily hands were oars enough,
Their tillers were their tails.

Four corners to my bed

Four corners to my bed,
Four angels round my head
One to watch and two to pray,
One to keep all fears away.

Hey-how for Hallowe'en

Hey-how for Hallowe'en
A' the witches to be seen;
Some black and some green,
Hew-how for Hallowe'en.

I saw a ship a-sailing

I saw a ship a-sailing,
A-sailing on the sea;
And, oh! it was all laden
With pretty things for thee!

There were comfits in the cabin,
And apples in the hold
The sails were made of silk,
And the masts were made of gold.

The four-and-twenty sailors
That stood between the decks,
Were four-and-twenty white mice
With chains about their necks.

The captain was a duck,
With a packet on his back;
And when the ship began to move,
The captain said, 'Quack! quack!'

If you sneeze on Monday

If you sneeze on Monday, you sneeze for danger;
Sneeze on a Tuesday, kiss a stranger;
Sneeze on a Wednesday, sneeze for a letter;
Sneeze on a Thursday, something better;
Sneeze on a Friday, sneeze for sorrow;
Sneeze on a Saturday, see your sweetheart to-morrow.

Jing-a-Ring

Here we go round the jing-a-ring,
Jing-a-ring, jing-a-ring;
Here we go round the jing-a-ring,
About the merry-matanzie.

Twice about, and then we fall,
Then we fall, then we fall,
Twice about and then we fall,
About the merry-matanzie.

Guess you who the goodman is,
Goodman is, goodman is,
Guess you who the goodman is,
About the merry matanzie.

Honey is sweet, and so is he,
So is he, so is he,
Honey is sweet and so is he,
About the merry-matanzie.

He's married with a gay gold ring,
A gay gold ring, a gay gold ring;
He's married with a gay gold ring,
About the merry-matanzie.

Now they're married, we'll wish them joy,
Wish them joy, wish them joy;
Now they're married we'll wish them joy,
About the merry-matanzie.

Father and mother they must obey,
Must obey, must obey,
Father and mother they must obey,
About the merry-matanzie.

Loving each other like brother and sister,
Sister and brother, sister and brother,
Loving each other like sister and brother,
About the merry-matanzie.

We pray the couple to kiss together,
Kiss together, kiss together,
We pray the couple to kiss together,
About the merry-matanzie.

Girls' singing game

Katie Beardie

Katie Beardie had a cow,
Black and white about the mou, *mouth*
Wasna that a dainty cow?
Dance Katie Beardie!

Katie Beardie had a hen,
Cackled but and cackled ben, *outside, inside*
Wasna that a dainty hen?
Dance Katie Beardie!

Katie Beardie had a cock,
That could spin, and bake, and rock,
Wasna that a dainty cock?
Dance Katie Beardie!

Katie Beardie had a grice, *a young pig*
It could skate upon the ice,
Wasna that a dainty grice?
Dance Katie Beardie!

Liar, liar, lick-spit

Liar, liar, lick-spit,
In ahint the candlestick!   *behind*
Whit's guid for awfu' liars?
Brimstane and muckle fires.

Matthew, Mark, Luke and John

Matthew, Mark, Luke and John,
Haud the cuddy til I loup on; *cow, jump*
Haud it fast and haud it sure,
Til I win owre the misty muir.

Och, here's a puir widow frae Babylon

Och, here's a puir widow frae Babylon,
Wi' six puir bairns a' alane;
Yin can bake, an' yin can brew,
Yin can shape, and yin can sew,
Yin can sit at the fire an' spin,
An' yin can bake a cake for the king;
Come pick ye east, come pick ye west,
An' pick the yin that ye loe the best.

Polly put the kettle on

Polly put the kettle on,
Polly put the kettle on,
Polly put the kettle on,
We'll all have tea.

Sukey take it off again,
Sukey take it off again,
Sukey take it off again,
They're all gone away.

The cuckoo is a bonnie bird

The cuckoo is a bonnie bird,
He sings clear as he flies;
He brings us all good tidings,
He tells us all nae lies.

He drinks the cold, cold water,
To keep his voice so clear;
And he will come again for sure
In the springtime of the year.

The Lion and the Unicorn

The lion and the unicorn
Fighting for the crown
Up jumps a wee dog
And knocks them both down.
Some got white bread,
And some got brown
But the lion beat the unicorn
All round the town.

There was a wee wifie rowed up in a blanket

There was a wee wifie rowed up in a blanket,   *rolled*
Nineteen times as high as the moon;
And what she did there I cannot declare,
For in her oxter she bore the sun.   *carried under her arm*

'Wee wifie, wee wifie, wee wifie,' quo I,
'What are you doing up there so high?'
'I'm blowing the cold clouds out of the sky.'
'Well done, well done, wee wifie,' quo I.

What are little boys made of?

What are little boys made of;
What are little boys made of?
'Snaps and snails, and puppy-dogs' tails;
And that's what little boys are made of.'

What are little girls made of, made of;
What are little girls made of?
'Sugar and spice, and all that's nice;
And that's what little girls are made of.'

Your plack and my plack

Your plack and my plack, *small coin worth ⅓ of a penny sterling*
Your plack and my plack,
Your plack and my plack,
And Jennie's bawbee. *a halfpenny*

We'll put them in the pint stoup, *drinking vessel*
Pint stoup, pint stoup,
We'll put them in the pint stoup,
And join all three.

And that was all my Jenny had,
My Jenny had, my Jenny had,
And all that my Jenny had,
Was a bawbee.

Four to Five

Aiken Drum

There was a man lived in the moon,
Lived in the moon, lived in the moon,
There was a man lived in the moon,
And his name was Aiken Drum.

Chorus
And he played upon a ladle,
A ladle, a ladle,
And he played upon a ladle,
and his name was Aiken Drum.

And his hat was made of good cream cheese,
Of good cream cheese, of good cream cheese,
And his hat was made of good cream cheese,
And his name was Aiken Drum.

And his coat was made of good roast beef,
Of good roast beef, of good roast beef,
And his coat was made of good roast beef,
And his name was Aiken Drum.

And his buttons made of penny loaves,
Of penny loaves, of penny loaves,
And his buttons made of penny loaves,
And his name was Aiken Drum.

And his waistcoat made of crust pies,
of crust pies, of crust pies,
And his waistcoat made of crust pies,
And his name was Aiken Drum.

And his breeches made of haggis bags,
Of haggis bags, of haggis bags,
And his breeches made of haggis bags,
And his name was Aiken Drum.

A nonsense adaptation for children from an old eighteenth century Jacobite song written after the Battle of Sheriffmuir (1715)

As I went o'er the Hill o' Hoos

As I went o'er the Hill o' Hoos,
I met a bonnie flock o' doos;   *doves*
They were a' nick-nackit,
They were a' brown-backit;
Sic a bonnie flock o' doos,
Comin' o'er the Hill o' Hoos.

Blaw, blaw!

Blaw, blaw!
Sic a day amang the dockens!
Blaw, Willie Buckthorn!
A' the sheip's i' the corn!

He that would thrive

He that would thrive
Must rise at five;
He that hath thriven
May lie till seven;
And he that by the plough would thrive,
Himself must either hold or drive.

How many miles to Glasgow Lea?

How many miles to Glasgow Lea?
Sixty, seventy, eighty-three.

Will I be there by candle light?
Just if your legs be long and tight.

Open your gates and let me through!
Not without a beck and a bow.

There's your beck and there's your bow,   *curtsey*
Open your gates and let me through!

I had three little sisters across the sea

I had three little sisters across the sea,
Peerie, weerie, winkum, do, re, me;
What handsome presents they all sent me,
Pinkum, quartum, Paradise lost them,
Peerie, weerie, winkum, do, re, me.

The first was a chicken without a bone,
Peerie, weerie, winkum, do, re, me;
The second was a cherry without a stone,
Pinkum, quartum, Paradise lost them,
Peerie, weerie, winkum, do, re, me.

The third was a blanket without a thread,
Peerie, weerie, winkum, do, re, me;
The fourth was a book that couldn't be read,
Pinkum, quartum, Paradise lost them,
Peerie, weerie, winkum, do, re, me.

How could there be a chicken without a bone?
Peerie, weerie, winkum, do, re, me;
How could there be a cherry without a stone?
Pinkum, quartum, Paradise lost them,
Peerie, weerie, winkum, do, re, me.

How could there be a blanket without a thread?
Peerie, weerie, winkum, do, re, me;
How could there be a book that couldn't be read?
Pinkum, quartum, Paradise lost them,
Peerie, weerie, winkum, do, re, me.

The chicken in the egg without a bone,
Peerie, weerie, winkum, do, re, me;
The cherry in the blossom without a stone,
Pinkum, quartum, Paradise lost them,
Peerie, weerie, winkum, do, re, me.

The blanket in the fleece without a thread,
Peerie, weerie, winkum, do, re, me;
The book in the press that couldn't be read,
Pinkum, quartum, Paradise lost them,
Peerie, weerie, winkum, do, re, me.

If the evening's red, and the morning gray

If the evening's red, and the morning gray,
It is the sign of a bonnie day;
If the evening's gray, and the morning red,
The lamb and the ewe will go wet to bed.

Mary had a little lamb

Mary had a little lamb,
Its fleece was white as snow
And everywhere that Mary went,
The lamb was sure to go.

It followed her to school one day,
It was against the rule,
And made the children laugh and play,
To see a lamb at school.

And so the teacher turned it out
But still it lingered near
And waited patiently about
'Til Mary did appear.

'What makes the lamb love Mary so?'
The eager children cry,
'Why Mary loves the lamb, you know!'
The teacher did reply.

This is a nursery rhyme which travelled across the Atlantic to Scotland. It was first published in Boston and was inspired by a young girl, Mary Sawyer (later Mrs Mary Tyler) who kept a pet lamb, which she took to school one day at the suggestion of her brother.

The moon shines bright (and girls and boys, come out to play)

The moon shines bright,
And the stars gie a light,
We'll see to kiss a bonny lass
At ten o'clock at night.

Moon, moon,
Mak' me a pair o' shoon,
And I'll dance till ye be done.

Lazy deuks, that sit i' the coal-neuks,   *ducks, coal-hole*
And winna come out to play;
Leave your supper, and leave your sleep,
Come out and play at hide-and-seek.

The version of the same rhyme south of the border was

Girls and boys, come out to play;
The moon doth shine as bright as day;
Leave your supper, and leave your sleep,
And come with your playfellows into the street.
Come with a whoop, come with a call,
Come with a good will or not at all.
Up the ladder and down the wall,
A halfpenny roll will serve us all.
You find milk, and I'll find flour,
And we'll have a pudding in half-an-hour.

My wheelie goes round

My wheelie goes round,
My wheelie goes round,
And my wheelie she casts the band,
It's not my wheelie that has the wit,
It's my uncanny hand.

This is a rhyme from the olden days when girls spun wool on a spinning wheel to get it ready for knitting.

Old Mother Hubbard

Old Mother Hubbard
Went to the cupboard
To get her poor dog a bone;
But when she came there
The cupboard was bare,
And so the poor dog had none.

She went to the baker's
To buy him some bread,
But when she came back
The poor dog was dead.

She went to the joiner's
To buy him a coffin,
But when she came back
The poor dog was laughing.

She took a clean dish
To get him some tripe,
But when she came back
He was smoking his pipe.

She went to the fishmonger's
To buy him some fish.
And when she came back
He was licking the dish.

She went to the ale-house
To get him some beer,
But when she came back
The dog sat in a chair.

She went to the tavern
For white wine and red,
But when she came back
The dog stood on his head.

She went to the hatter's
To buy him a hat,
But when she came back
He was feeding the cat.

She went to the barber's
To buy him a wig,
But when she came back
He was dancing a jig.

She went to the fruiterer's
To buy him some fruit,
But when she came back
He was playing the flute.

She went to the tailor's
To buy him a coat,
But when she came back
He was riding a goat.

She went to the cobbler's
To buy him some shoes,
But when she came back
He was reading the news.

She went to the sempstress
To buy him some linen,
But when she came back
The dog was spinning.

She went to the hosier's
To buy him some hose,
But when she came back
He was dress'd in his clothes.

The dame made a curtsey,
The dog made a bow;
The dame said, 'Your servant,'
The dog said, 'Bow, wow.'

Paddy on the Railway

Paddy on the railway
Picking up stones;
Along came an engine
And broke poor Paddy's bones.

'O!' said Paddy,
'That's not fair.'
'O!' said the engineman,
'You shouldna have been there!'

Sticks and Stones

Sticks and stones
Will break my bones,
But names will never hurt me.

When I'm dead,
And in my grave,
You'll be sorry for what you called me!

Simple Simon met a Pieman

Simple Simon met a pieman
Going to the Fair,
Said Simple Simon to the pieman
Let me taste your ware.

Says the pieman to Simple Simon,
Show me first your penny;
Says Simple Simon to the pieman,
Indeed I have not any.

Simple Simon went a-fishing,
For to catch a whale;
All the water he had got,
Was in his mother's pail.

Simple Simon went to look
If plums grew on a thistle;
He pricked his fingers very much,
Which made poor Simon whistle.

This rhyme goes back to Elizabethan times in the sixteenth century although it was not published until 1764.

The Frog and Mouse

There lived a Puddy in a well,   *puddock – frog*
Cuddy alone, cuddy alone;
There lived a Puddy in a well,
Cuddy alone and I.
There was a Puddy in a well,
And a mousie in a mill;
Kickmaleerie, cowden down,
Cuddy alone and I.

Puddy he'd a-wooin' ride,
Sword and pistol by his side.

Puddy came to the mouse's wonne: *dwelling*
'Mistress Mouse, are you within?'

'Yes, kind sir, I am within;
Saftly do I sit and spin.'

'Madam, I am come to woo;
Marriage I must have of you.'

'Marriage I will grant you nane,
Till Uncle Rottan he comes hame.' *rat*

Uncle Rottan's now come hame,
Fye, gar busk the bride alang. *make ready*

Lord Rottan sat at the head o' the table,
Because he was baith stout and able.

Wha is't that sits next the wa',
But Lady Mouse, baith jimp and sma'? *neat*

Wha is't that sits next the bride,
But the sola Puddy wi' his yellow side? *cheerful*

Syne came the Deuk but and the Drake,
The Deuk took the Puddy, and gart him squaik.

Then came in the carle Cat,
Wi' a fiddle on his back:
Want ye ony music here?

The Puddy he swam down the brook,
The Drake he catched him in his fluke.

The Cat he pu'd Lord Rottan down,
The kittlins they did claw his crown.

But Lady Mouse, baith jimp and sma',
Crept into a hole beneath the wa';
'Squeak!' quo' she, 'I'm weel awa'.

The Raven and the Crow

The corbie with his roupie throat   *hoarse*
Cried frae the leafless tree,
'Come o'er the loch, come o'er the loch,
Come o'er the loch wi me!'

The craw put out his sooty head,
And cried, 'Whaur tae, whaur tae?'
'To yonder field,' the corbie cried,
'Where there is corn enow.'

'The ploughman ploughed the land yestreen,
The farmer sowed this morn,
And we can mak a full fat meal,
From off the broadcast corn.'

The twa black birds flew o'er the trees,
They flew towards the sun;
The farmer watching by the hedge
Shot baith with his lang gun.

Tom, Tom, the Piper's Son

Tom, Tom, the piper's son,
Stole a pig and away he run
Pig was eat, and Tom was beat,
And Tom went roaring down the street.

The 'pig' mentioned in the song is not a live animal but a kind of pastry smaller than a pie, often made with an apple filling.

Another version of the rhyme is:

Tom, Tom, the piper's son,
Stole a pig, and away he run.
Tom run here, Tom run there,
Tom run through the village square.

This rhyme is often blended with a separate and longer rhyme:

Tom, he was a piper's son,
He learnt to play when he was young,
And all the tune that he could play
Was 'over the hills and far away';
Over the hills and a great way off,
The wind shall blow my top-knot off.
Tom with his pipe made such a noise,
That he pleased both the girls and boys,
They all stopped to hear him play,
'Over the hills and far away'.

Tom with his pipe did play with such skill
That those who heard him could never keep still;
As soon as he played they began for to dance,
Even the pigs on their hind legs would after him prance.
As Dolly was milking her cow one day,
Tom took his pipe and began to play;
So Dolly and the cow danced 'The Cheshire Round',
Till the pail was broken and the milk ran on the ground.

He met old Dame Trot with a basket of eggs,
He used his pipe and she used her legs;
She danced about till the eggs were all broke,
She began for to fret, but he laughed at the joke.
Tom saw a cross fellow was beating an ass,
Heavy laden with pots, pans, dishes, and glass;
He took out his pipe and he played them a tune,
And the poor donkey's load was lightened full soon.

The origin of the shorter verse is lost in the mists of time but the longer poem was first published in 1795.

Rhymes about the weather

When cocks gang crawin' to their beds

When cocks gang crawin' to their beds,
They'll rise in the morn wi' watery heads.

When the wind is in the east

When the wind is in the east
'Tis neither good for man nor beast;
When the wind is in the north,
The skilful fisher goes not forth;
When the wind is in the south,
It blows the bait in the fishes' mouth;
When the wind is in the west,
Then 'tis at the very best.

When Yule comes, dule comes

When Yule comes, dule comes,   *Christmas*
Cauld feet and legs;
When Pasch comes, grace comes,   *Easter & spring*
Butter, milk and eggs.

Five to Six

A man of words and not of deeds

A man of words and not of deeds,
Is like a garden full of weeds,
And when the weeds begin to grow,
It's like a garden full of snow;
And when the snow begins to fall,
It's like a bird upon the wall;
And when the bird away does fly,
It's like an eagle in the sky;
And when the sky begins to roar,
It's like a lion at the door;
And when the door begins to crack,
It's like a stick across your back;
And when your back begins to smart,
It's like a penknife in your heart;
And when your heart begins to bleed,
You're dead, and dead, and dead, indeed.

Bless the sheep for Dauvid's sake

Bless the sheep for Dauvid's sake, he herdit sheep himsel;
Bless the fish for Peter's sake, he gruppit fish himsel;
Bless the soo for Satan's sake, he was yince a soo himsel.

If wishes were horses

If wishes were horses,
Beggars would ride;
If turnips were watches,
I would wear one by my side.

March said to Averil

March said to Averil:
'I see three hoggs on yonder hill;   *young sheep*
And if you'll lend me dayis three,
I'll find a way to gar them die!'
The first o' them was wind and weet;
The second o' them was snaw and sleet;
The third o' them was sic a freeze,
It froze the birds' feet to the trees.
When the three days were past and gane,
The silly poor hoggs came hirpling hame.

St Swithin's day, if thou dost rain

St Swithin's day, if thou dost rain,
For forty days it will remain:
St. Swithin's day, if thou be fair,
For forty days 'twill rain na mair.

See a pin and pick it up

See a pin and pick it up,
All the day you'll have good luck;
See a pin and let it lay,
Bad luck you'll have all the day!

Tam o' the Linn

Tam o' the linn came up the gate,   *waterfall*
With twenty puddings on a plate,
And each pudding had a pin,   *fastening*
'We'll eat them all,' quo Tam o' the linn.

Tam o' the linn had no breeks to wear,
He bought a sheepskin to make him a pair,
The fleshy side out, the woolly side in,
'It's fine summer clothing,' quo Tam o' the linn.

Tam o' the linn, he had three bairns,
They fell in the fire in each other's arms;
'Oh,' quo the last one, 'I've got a hot skin.'
'It's hotter below,' said Tam o' the linn.

Tam o' the linn went to the moss,
To seek a stable to his horse;
The moss was open, and Tam fell in,
'I've stabled myself,' quo Tam o' the linn.

The Fause Knicht

'O, where are you going?'
Quo the fause knicht upon the road;
'I'm going to the school.'
Quo the wee boy, and still he stood.

'What is that upon your back?'
Quo the fause knicht upon the road; *false*
'Ah well, it is my books,'
Quo the wee boy, and still he stood.

'What's that you've under your arm?'
Quo the fause knicht upon the road.
'Ah well, it is my peat,'
Quo the wee boy, and still he stood.

'Who's acht they sheep?'
Quo the fause knicht upon the road,
'They're mine and my mother's,'
Quo the wee boy, and still he stood.

'How many of them are mine?'
Quo the fause knicht upon the road.
'All they that have blue tails,'
Quo the wee boy, and still he stood.

'I wish you were on yon tree,'
Quo the fause knicht upon the road,
'And a good ladder under me,'
Quo the wee boy, and still he stood.

'And the ladder for to break,'
Quo the fause knicht upon the road.
'And for you to fall down,'
Quo the wee boy, and still he stood.

'I wish you were in yon sea,'
Quo the fause knicht upon the road;
'And a good coble under me,'
Quo the wee boy, and still he stood.

'And the coble for to break,'
Quo the fause knicht upon the road.
'And you to be drowned,'
Quo the wee boy, and still he stood.

The Fishermen's Song

O blithely shines the bonnie sun
Upon the Isle of May,
And blithely rolls the morning tide
Into St Andrew's bay.

When haddocks leave the Firth of Forth,
And mussels leave the shore,
When oysters climb up Berwick Law,
We'll go to sea no more,
No more,
We'll go to sea no more.

The gunpowder plot

The gunpowder plot
Will ne'er be forgot
While Edinburgh Castle
Stands on a rock.

A cry of Edinburgh boys in the days when the guns of Edinburgh Castle were fired on November the fifth.

The Wee, Wee Man

As I was walking all alane,
Atween a water and a wa,
O there I met a wee, wee man,
And he was the least I ever saw.

His legs were scarce a shathmont lang, *a fist with the thumb extended*
And thick and thimber was his thigh; *heavy*
Atween his brows there was a span,
And atween his shouthers there was three.

And he took up a muckle stane,
And flung it as far as I could see;
Though I had been the Wallace wight,
I couldna lift it to my knee.

'O, wee, wee man, but thou be strang!
O, tell me where thy dwelling be!'
'My dwelling's down at yon bonny bower,
O, will you gang with me and see?'

On we lap, and away we rade,
Till we came to yon bonny green;
We lighted down to bait our horse,
And out there cam a lady fine.

Four-and-twenty at her back,
And they were all clad out in green;
Though the King of Scotland had been there
The worst of them might have been his queen.

And on we lap, and away we rade,
Till we cam to yon bonny hall,
Where the roof was of the beaten gold,
And the floor was of the crystal all.

And there were harpings loud and sweet,
And ladies dancing jimp and small; *slender*
But in the twinkling of an eye,
My wee, wee man was clean awa.

They that wash on Monanday

They that wash on Monanday,
Hae a' the week to dry;
They that wash on Tyesday,
Are no' far by.
They that wash on Wednesday,
Are no sair to mean;
They that wash on Thursday,
May get their claes clean.
They that wash on Friday,
Hae gey meikle need;
They that wash on Saturday,
Are dirty daws indeed! *Fuel made of cow-dung and coal dust*

This is the way we go to school

This is the way we go to school,
Go to school, go to school,
This is the way go to school,
On a cold and frosty morning

This is the way we come out of school,
Come out of school, come out of school,
This is the way we come out of school
On a cold and frosty morning.

When good King David ruled this land

When good King David ruled this land,
He was a goodly king;
He took three pecks of barley-meal,
To make a bag-pudding.

A bag-pudding the king did make,
And stuffed it well with plums.
And in it put great lumps of fat,
As big as my two thumbs.

The king and queen did eat thereof,
And noblemen beside;
And what they could not eat that night,
The queen next morning fried.

When I was a wee thing

When I was a wee thing
'Bout six or seven year auld
I had no worth a petticoat,
To keep me frae the cauld.

Then I went to Edinburgh,　　　　　　　　*burgh*
To bonnie burrows town,　　　　　　　　*bought*
And there I coft a petticoat,　　　　　　*short skirt*
A kirtle, and a gown.

As I cam hame again,
I thought I wad big a kirk,　　　　　　　*build*
And a' the fowls o' the air
Wad help me wi' the work.

The heron, wi' her lang neb,
She moupit me the stanes;   *dropped*
The doo, wi' her rough legs,
She led me them hame.

The gled he was a wily thief,   *buzzard or kite*
He rackled up the wa';
The pyat was a curst thief,   *magpie*
She dang down a'.

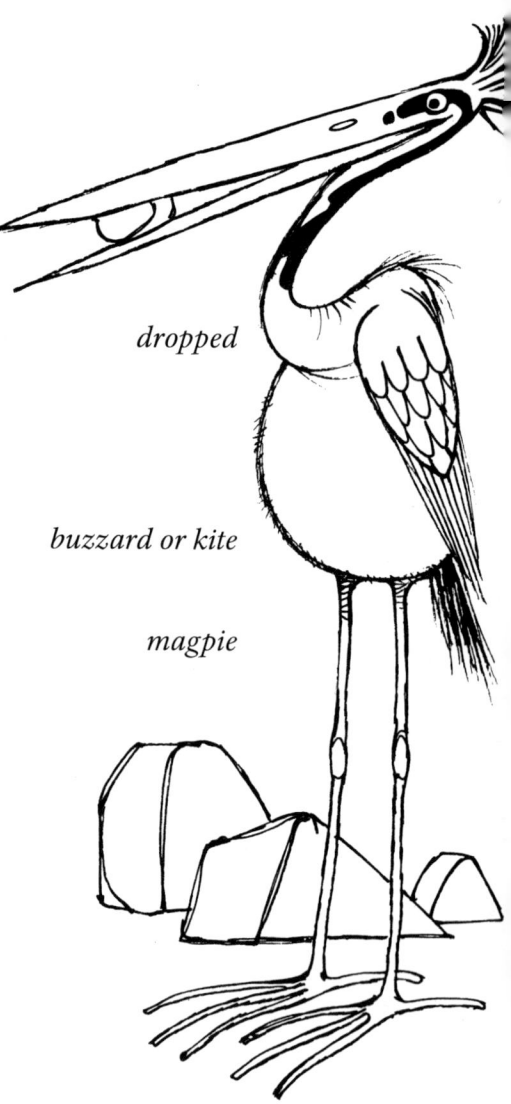

The hare came hirpling owre the knowe,
To ring the morning bell;
The hurcheon she came after,   *hedgehog*
And said she wad do't hersel.

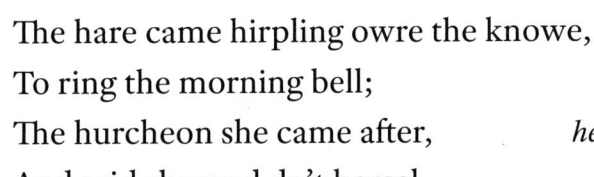

The herring was the high priest,
The salmon was the clerk,
The howlet read the order—
They held a bonnie wark.

Wild geese, wild geese

Wild geese, wild geese, ganging to the sea,
Good weather it will be.
Wild geese, wild geese, ganging to the hill,
The weather it will spill.

Luath Press Limited
committed to publishing well written books worth reading

LUATH PRESS takes its name from Robert Burns, whose little collie Luath (*Gael.*, swift or nimble) tripped up Jean Armour at a wedding and gave him the chance to speak to the woman who was to be his wife and the abiding love of his life. Burns called one of 'The Twa Dogs' Luath after Cuchullin's hunting dog in Ossian's *Fingal*. Luath Press was established in 1981 in the heart of Burns country, and now resides a few steps up the road from Burns' first lodgings on Edinburgh's Royal Mile.

Luath offers you distinctive writing with a hint of unexpected pleasures.

Most bookshops in the UK, the US, Canada, Australia, New Zealand and parts of Europe either carry our books in stock or can order them for you. To order direct from us, please send a £sterling cheque, postal order, international money order or your credit card details (number, address of cardholder and expiry date) to us at the address below. Please add post and packing as follows: UK – £1.00 per delivery address; overseas surface mail – £2.50 per delivery address; overseas airmail – £3.50 for the first book to each delivery address, plus £1.00 for each additional book by airmail to the same address. If your order is a gift, we will happily enclose your card or message at no extra charge.

Luath Press Limited
543/2 Castlehill
The Royal Mile
Edinburgh EH1 2ND
Scotland

Telephone: 0131 225 4326 (24 hours)
email: sales@luath.co.uk
Website: www.luath.co.uk